Around the World We Go!

Sandy Creek
NEW YORK

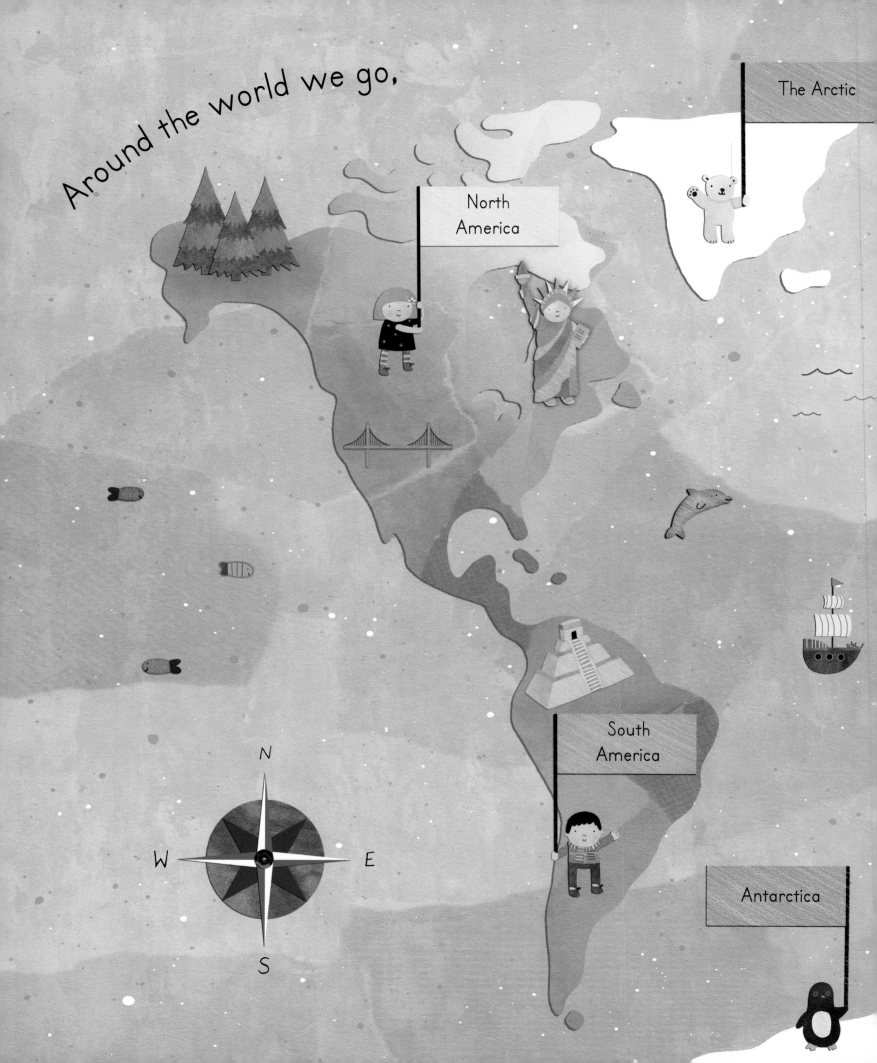

Europe

Asia

Africa

Australia

To learn what we don't know.

In foreign lands,

We'll all

shake
hands,

As around the world we go!

Around the
world we go,

To learn what we don't know.

We'll make our eyes
A great big size

To see
what we
don't know.

Around the world we go,

Each language we don't know.

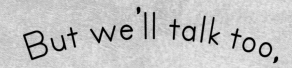
But we'll talk too,

Comment ça va?

¿Cómo estás?

How are you?

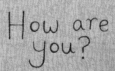

Around the world we go,

In singing we can show

A way to play

In a friendly way,

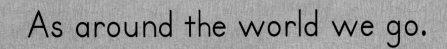

As around the world we go.

Around the world we go,

The world is rather slow,

Because we run

ahead of the world,

As around
we

the world go!

Sandy Creek
NEW YORK

An Imprint of Sterling Publishing
387 Park Avenue South
New York, NY 10016

ISBN 978-1-4351-4720-1

Manufactured in Heshan, China
Lot #:
10 9 8 7 6 5 4 3 2 1

04/13